SAMBA-CANÇÃO

Eduardo Borsato

SAMBA-CANÇÃO

1st Edition
POD

Petrópolis
KBR
2012

Text edition **KBR**
Translation **A.H. Lin**
Cover **KBR**

Copyright © 2012 *Eduardo Borsato*
All rights reserved

ISBN: 978-85-8180-193-3

KBR Editora Digital Ltda.
www.kbrdigital.com.br
atendimento@kbrdigital.com.br
55|24|2222.3491

B869 - Brazilian Literature

Printed in Brazil

**Eduardo Borsato** is a playwright, novelist and short stories author. He has worked as a ghostwriter; he was a television scriptwriter for TV Globo, where he adapted soap opera texts for books and pocket books. For 10 years he was the editor of house organs and neighborhood newspapers. He has published *My Daughter Also* and other short stories with KBR.

Website: http://www.eduardo.borsato.nom.br/
E-mail: contato@eduardo.borsato.nom.br

To Alírio Gonçalves de Carvalho Filho

I'm tired of riding the horse of pretension
I still can't even make myself a human being.

Elias Canetti

TABLE OF CONTENTS

THE DREAM

Clementina always dreamt of having a broken bone—an arm, a leg—ah, the pleasure of a compound fracture, preferably with the bone exposed.

As a child, she tried everything: riding a scooter with her eyes closed (it was long ago, even before skateboards existed), throwing herself in front of a bus on Cesario de Melo Avenue, spitting in her oldest brother's eye.

Nothing worked. She went through childhood feeling deeply disappointed.

As an adolescent she consoled herself by becoming a *connoisseur* of accident victims, any type—from those run down in traffic, to second and third-degree burn victims, not to mention those killed during crimes of passion, executed by the militia, and assorted anonymous corpses. A burial never took place without her, she never missed a wake or a funeral mass.

But none of this satisfied her; and that was her state, unsatisfied, when she fell in love.

The engagement

"Prove that you love me. Throw me under a car," she begged her boyfriend, actually now her fiancé after six months of dating and with the wedding date set.

Godofredo—or Godo, as he was called—possessed a bovine peacefulness and was incapable of killing a fly.

"Then hit me in the face with your fist. Hard. Knock out my teeth, my front teeth."

And he, indignant, said, "I'm not a bastard. Only a bastard would hit the woman he loved. Only a bastard."

Rich, the owner of a chain of paint stores, The Golden Paintbrush, had already planned their honeymoon to New York.

"Ay, Godo! Fifteen days in New York?! It is too much, too much!"

And, coyly, Clementina added, "Won't you be ashamed of me?"

"Ashamed?"

"I am a country bumpkin. I've never been out of Campo Grande. I barely speak Portuguese, whereas you...are traveled...speak English,

French."

"You make me happy. What else matters?"

She smacks his cheek with a kiss:

"Ay, Godo!"

He smiled, humbled. Her enthusiasm disguised the frustration that her dream would not come true. If everyone else could have their dream realized, why not her?

The wedding

Godo bought a small condo at the Sunflower Park apartment building. Clementina only made one categorical demand: "It must have a staircase. Without a handrail."

He took care of everything: furniture, new clothes, a complete trousseau, one for him and one for her. Clementina looked at everything and could not believe her eyes. The daughter of a modest couple, she was delighted with the fine clothes, the expensive shoes. "Good-bye poverty!"

Since they were not religious, a Justice of the Peace performed the wedding in a very simple ceremony. The reception, on the other hand, was grand, held at Rei do Gado[1], the most charming grange in Campo Grande, on the Es-

---

1 "King of Livestock"

trada da Grama.[2]

Now they had only to go home, change clothes, cab to the airport, and...

"Take me in your arms."

He lifted her, carried her up the stairs. On the last step, he tripped, and they sprawled on the floor.

The following day, the front-page headline of the newspaper, *The Yellow,* read, typo and all: "A serious accident almost cutes down the life of newlyweds."

Godo only dislocated his shoulder, but Clementina broke both legs with—oh glorious heavens—an exposed fracture of the right.

Those who went to visit her at the Our Lady de Carmo Hospital found the patient in a cast from the waist down, almost unable to move, but smiling, happy as a hawk that had just found a nest of baby birds.

---

2 Street of Grass

The kiss

Between classes, two teachers talk.

"Elisa's problem is that..."

"What? She has a problem?"

"You've never noticed?"

"Go on."

"Inferiority complex."

"What?"

"She thinks her cake won't rise."

"Truly?"

"What's more, she says that living on the outskirts is punishment."

"Wait a minute. Wasn't she born in Corcundinha?"

"She was."

"That's right. A neighborhood of Campo Grande."

"You see? Punished. Twofold. A double dose. Huge. And there's more..."

They exposed the life of Elisa there on the school patio with the noonday sun shining as if it were a pound of rump roast sliced by a blood-stained butcher: her father, a bus conductor, earned a miserable wage; her illiterate mother barely earned anything as a cleaning woman; Elisa and her three siblings had been raised in a shack with only one room; she, a clerk at a dollar store, went to night school to become a teacher, taking the qualifying test three times before she passed.

"Greek tragedy! Pure Greek tragedy!"

And the other teacher says in a sad voice, "Tell me about it."

It was only a matter of time before Elisa would become a complete pessimist, the stupidity, the students' disrespectful apathy, their insults, all fueling her depressed personality. What is more—she took it as a personal offense. She left the classroom willing to enter the first corner bar she saw and have a shot of guarana with rat poison.

"Deep down she is a pure soul. The best. She only wants to be accepted, to please."

The other teacher took a deep breath, tersely adding:

"Now, my daughter, it would be a miracle."

SAMBA-CANÇÃO

The miracle

Bakery flies. Her, the cake. The students surrounded her, pulled, fawned. Sophia Loren in the arms of Marcelo Mastroianni; Sharon Stone in the arms of Michael Douglas, or, more Brazilian, Virginia Lane in the arms of President Getulio, or...

She was floating in the clouds. And she really was, sort of. In almost ten years of teaching, this was the first time that...

A friend, another teacher, entered the classroom.

"Have you lost your mind?"

Before she could respond, the teacher pulled her into the bathroom:

"Look in the mirror!"

She looked.

"What's wrong?"

She usually went without a bra. And on that day...

The friend grew more accusatory:

"This blouse. It's transparent, your nipples..."

A pair of breasts, nipples showing, was it cause for such a scandal? The other teacher dramatically extended a sheet of paper.

"What's this?"

"A letter. Anonymous. It's gone through the whole school. The principal has already seen it."

The letter said that she was in love with one of her students and on *that* day in *that* class she would teach wearing *that* blouse with her nipples showing because *that* student had asked her to, and it was Thursday, and every Thursday the two had sex in the employee's bathroom and...

"You aren't saying that..."

"I am."

"They believed it?"

"Everyone."

"You?"

"Everyone."

"The principal?"

"Everyone, I told you."

In disgust, she replied:

"Slander! The blouse? Pure coincidence! To have sex?! A lie!"

Raising her voice further:

"Do you want to know? Do you want to know?"

The fatal revelation followed:

"I am a virgin!" she repeated, almost yelling.

"A virgin, you hear? A virgin!"

The other teacher laughed in scorn, "At

thirty-five?"

"A Virgin!"

"Prove it!"

She jumped. "What?"

"Get a gynecological exam. Would you agree to it?" After a brief silence, she added, "It is the only way. Agreed?"

Elisa lowers her eyes, understanding everything—the favors from students, male students, the withdrawn girls with their secretive giggles. Bastards, a mob of bastards. Witch hunt. The staff preferred to believe them, even her friend...

She was unbearably lost. The world was turning its back on her, and she would turn her back on the world. Her death would be her revenge. She would put an end to an existence that was no longer worth living. Her sacrifice would not be in vain. Like the wrongly accused Joan of Arc, she would die—in the outskirts of the city—but like Joan of Arc just the same.

She would leave life in order to enter history.[3] At least the history of Campo Grande.

The suicide

---

3 Famous line from the suicide note of President Getulio, a dictator of Brazil in the early fifties.

At home, bent over, bewildered, she realized that she did not thoroughly understand the incident at school. Plus, to her, suicide had never been anything more than a vague abstraction, a metaphysical possibility at best.

She remembered her father's death and mother's death, the wake, the bodies, the prayers, the crying. Clearly, being dead, she would be spared this vision. But, what the hell, even as an inert empty shell, it was still her body, unmercifully exposed at the cemetery.

Finally, the decisive argument: Could anyone guarantee that she would be unable to smell the flowers, the candles, the sweet odor of the grim reaper's morbid breath? It goes without saying, they would undress her, wash her, scrub her, her intimate parts shamelessly exposed!

No, no! She rejected that Calvary with all her might. But, if she didn't accept physical death, she could very well die on the inside, to rot internally, to kill her connection to the world, to have a beautiful, odorless, aseptic moral death.

Resolved on this crucial point, she disconnected her telephone, her computer, the gas, shooed away her pet cat, locked the front door, drew the bedroom curtain, and lied down. She was bidding good-bye to this ungrateful life and entering another, not shared with anyone beyond herself, filled with manna of the gods. Lulled by such profound purposes, she fell asleep.

The surprise

Two or three hours later, she awoke to stabbing hunger pangs. This prosaic, physical contingency forced her to turn on the light, open the refrigerator, heat some food, and return to life.

On her computer, her email inbox contained a message from an unidentified sender. She opened it. She got a rude shock. It said, "My love. I will be waiting for you tonight at 8:00 at the Gaucho Spit barbecue which is very close to the cultural zone at the entrance to Campinho Street. I only ask one thing of you: Wear the same blouse you wore in school today. Do you remember? The one that showed your nipples. Super, super sensual. When you arrive, I will give you a kiss on the right cheek. By this kiss you will know me. Don't forget: Tonight at 8:00. Eternally in love with you."

Were they trying to drive her crazy? Hadn't enough happened at school: the near-suicide, her penance, the herculean effort to return to life, her way of the cross? Wasn't it enough? She ranted, stifling an outraged scream.

Without conscious planning, she lifted

her finger. She intended to lower it toward the *delete* button to free herself from the torture, to shut out once and for all that which...

The kiss

She couldn't stop herself from reading the message one last time. It contained grammatical mistakes, not too bad, but mistakes just the same. Slight ones, in fact, but...

Bollocks! Who would have written it? Even if she took the mistakes into account, none of her students would be able to. If they couldn't have written it, the male teachers could have, or the female teachers. Or could it be someone from outside the school? Damn! Who?

By the time she realized what had happened, she had already taken a bath, dressed in that very blouse which she hid discretely under a sweater, and checked her watch. She lived on Monteiro Road, so the Gaucho Spit was not far. All she needed to do was to get a cab and...

It was a clear night with a starry sky. From atop the viaduct she could see a train, the buildings far in the distance, lights burning, the traffic jam in the lane that came from the city. For the first time she was enjoying herself, feeling accepted and cared for, awash in a peaceful feeling.

Smiling slightly, she could not stop thinking that not so long ago she envisioned herself as Joan of Arc reborn. Well, now she felt more like Christ himself. Was she not, like him, on the way to an encounter with a kiss on the cheek? Then what?

Except that she had a sizable advantage over the son of God. Whereas Judas' kiss had wickedly betrayed him, hers remained a warm mystery. It could come from a Judas in the form of a colleague, someone anonymous, even a dyke. But it could just as well be an angel who would bring her redemption, who would take her virginity in exchange for professions of love, of the deepest passion. Or, who knows...

With a sigh, she jumped out of the taxi and entered the barbecue.

SAMBA-CANÇÃO[4]

He could never accept Isabel's wedding. The most coveted girl in Belisario dos Santos High School, candidate for Miss Campo Grande—not elected due to the quintessential stupidity of the judges—was always flirting with him. In just a short leap, they were dating.

"He is the luckiest guy in the world!" grumbled his classmates, purple with envy.

Then she suddenly met Machado. They married in six months. Passions boiling, she didn't even finish her studies.

"She is going to realize she made a big mistake. Young, pretty, highly doable—one could hardly guess what happened!"

But feeling the pain of the spurned lover, he knew very well that nothing happened, except...

---

4 Literally "Samba Song," a sad and romantic old musical genre; but it is a double entendre and also refers to old-fashioned long briefs worn by Brazilian men.

"What was Machado's secret? What?"

The young widow

"Nothing," she responded. "If you are going to keep asking this, you can stop calling me."

"There must be something. There must."

"Did you hear me? Rehashing. I'm going to hang up."

"Don't do it. Don't..."

Her Calvary appeared to have no end. After the wedding, she and Machado had moved to Bangu. He was a wholesaler on the grocery-and-liquor-store circuit—the worst wholesaler there was, by the way.

"He went into bankruptcy. It put her in a very bad position," said Carvalhinho, the lawyer, in confidence. And, whispering into his ear said, "It was Machado's total incompetence. A huge loss. That's why he died."

Isabel, the widow, returned to Campo Grande.

"Living from hand to mouth. She rents an apartment. Without two pennies to rub together. She works to pay the bills," continued Carvalhinho. And, wetting his lips,

"But she's still hot. Stops traffic. Have you seen her?"

He not only saw her, he stalked her. Like a raving lunatic, he followed her footprints when she left work—she was an attendant in a medical office—and when she walked home. Isabel could not take a step without him following her like a bloodhound.

She, by the way, knew about it and allowed it. But she allowed it with an utterly condescending smile that killed him.

She sees me as a friend! Nothing more than a harmless friend! He ruminated while staring at the ceiling through the early-morning hours.

Then he would summon his conclusions which robbed him of his last hopes of sleep: "What was Machado's secret? What?"

The friend

With a frankness only allowed to be used by a close friend, a childhood friend, Sueli said to Isabel, "Are you going to stay a widow forever? Stop being a fool! Pay attention to Ederval."

"He's just a friend."

"He's obsessed with you. You don't see it because you don't want to."

"I'll say it again. He's just a friend."

"He's even willing to kill himself because of you. Keep your eyes open. Don't carry this cross."

"Eeek! Stop it. Are you blackmailing me?"

Isabel never guessed, but she had hit the nail on the head. Sueli had a hidden agenda. She was in love with Ederval herself. Her heart was stabbed by a crochet hook each time she saw him, and she ran into him every day.

She could not stand seeing him fall into disgrace for the love of another woman. "Why not me? Why not me?" she deliriously repeated.

Such frustration gave Sueli the morbid desire to get revenge, to tell him every small detail, to make him suffer, to compensate for her own suffering. For example, she told him that Isabel was horribly vain. She was always grimacing in the mirror, plastering her face with creams and rejuvenating salves, complaining that she didn't have enough money for plastic surgery.

At that point, Ederval was grinding his teeth, "I have taken a course in facial cosmetology! Diploma and all. I am the scalpless Pitangui[5] of Campo Grande!"

Then he yelled in pure frustration, "Why doesn't she come to me? Why?"

Adding to his suffering, Sueli whispered, "She has a room."

"A room?!"

---

5 An internationally acclaimed Brazilian plastic surgeon.

"A little room, locked tight as a drum. She doesn't let anyone in. I wonder what's inside." Sueli never tired of asking.

Isabel changed the subject:

"It's none of your business."

"What?" Ederval insisted, his voice strained with desperation to know.

Until one day, Isabel said, "I will only tell you one thing... so you will stop bugging me."

And Sueli said, "So, tell."

"A relic."

"What do you mean?"

"Of my Machado."

Ederval vented his misery with a pungent moan, "Is this how she treats the deceased?"

He found her *post mortem* intimacy of the lowest immorality.

"What relic?" insisted Sueli.

"That I cannot tell. Not even dead."

"She never said?" Ederval asked.

Sueli made a dismissive gesture, he looked away, with the utmost certainty that in that dark room, in that mysterious relic, the sacred secret of Machado was held.

The relic

The magazine said that Ana Maria Braga

and Xuxa[6] had done it.

"I don't know... Ana Maria Braga," said Sueli with a shudder.

"So what?"

"You don't know?"

"Tell me."

"Well, she looks all plastic. It doesn't count."

"And Xuxa?"

"As far as I know, only her breasts. Now, her face..."

She looked at Isabel. Perfect face, beautiful, not even the shadow of a wrinkle. Who would know she was pushing forty? *Ah, if mine could be like that*, she sighed, and wished to die.

"So? What do you think?"

The magazine told of a revolutionary treatment using chopped ice. One should dip her face in it, hold it down for three minutes, and it was done! Brand new skin, like a baby's butt, at the very least."

"What?" insisted Isabel.

"Do you have ice?"

"In the freezer. I bought it this morning."

"Go get it."

"So you think..."

"Damn it! Just get it. What are you wait-

---

6 Brazilian celebrities.

ing for?"

Everything prepared, before dipping her face in the ice, Isabel asked, "Will you keep track of the time?"

"What am I here for?"

Ah, if only she could keep her face immersed until she dropped dead, stiff and cold, and Sueli, finally free of that burden, that anguish, could make a pass at Ederval.

Suddenly, well before the three minutes was up, "Ouch!" groaned Isabel. She abruptly pushed away the basin of ice and raised her head.

"Ay!" yelled Sueli, frightened by the sight.

Isabel's mouth was twisted; her features, disfigured, the horror. Worse, she stopped breathing and collapsed on the floor as melodramatically as a silent screen actress.

Panicking—not completely sorry, but still somewhat sad to see her wishes granted so quickly—Sueli ran to ask for help from a neighbor on the floor above, who happened to be a retired nurse.

After examining Isabel she said, "She's not going to die. You can relax."

"But what was that...?"

"Does she have health insurance?"

"Who gives a rat's ass!"

"Let's put her in a cab and take her to Rocha Faria."

"Oh, my God!"

"You can chill out. Didn't I say she won't die?"

"So, then..."

"She needs to be put under observation. Because of her breathing."

"And the face?"

"It will return to normal after awhile."

"But..."

"Work with me here. I'll go with you, but you pay for the cab. You do have cash, don't you?"

As soon as Isabel recovered, Sueli regained her depravity and from the hospital called Ederval.

"I'm rushing over there!" he exclaimed in a thin voice, tightened by fear.

"Go to her apartment first."

"Why, for what?"

"The door is ajar."

"Listen, isn't it better..."

She almost yelled, "Go to the apartment. Don't you see?"

"What?"

"The room. The relic. This is our chance."

The light switch was behind the door. It took him a long time to find it. He waited for his eyes to adjust. The little room had no furniture, not even a miserable little stool. Where could it be?

That's when he spotted it: On one of the side walls, hanging high up almost to the ceiling. It was framed by a white backing and wide border to highlight the colors. It was white with gaudy red stripes.

The relic, at last.

That which maintained the flame lighting Isabel's heart, that which still burned her delicious flesh and left her drowning in memories that she could not confess"... nothing more than Machado's *samba-canção* boxer shorts.

Humiliated like a mouse in the sacristy, Ederval painfully squelched his sobs and hurried out, faced with the revolting awareness that he was worth less than a mere pair of underpants, placed in a more-than-questionable frame.

THE JUST MAN

During a coffee break he pulled his friend—pastor of the Universal[7]—to a corner of the counter and, feeling tortured, said:

"I feel like a prick, Terezo! A complete prick! How can I be forgiven?"

With the complacent, superior air of someone already saved, Terezo said:

"Repent, brother, it's half the battle."

"Do you know what worries me the most? Huh?" Not allowing Terezo to respond and cutting him off: "The other half of the battle."

"Trust. Jesus will guide you."

"And if he doesn't?"

"It will be the work of Satan."

"Who doesn't know that?"

"Then why do you doubt?"

Adalberto could only open his arms, pa-

---

7 A Christian evangelical church

thetic. He was so convinced of his own rascali-tythat he began to fear it.

In this state of mind Adalberto left his coffee half-drunk, turned his back on Terezo, and went out to the street. On the first corner, he ran into Justino.

The business associate

If Terezo's certainty of salvation made him a danger that Adalberto ought to avoid, Justino, on the other hand, exuded peace, the welcoming beatitude of a martyr. But Adalberto had spent the entire afternoon with this martyr's wife at the Agadir Motel in the center of Campo Grande.

"I am not going anywhere else. It has to take place at the Agadir." Luci was final about that: "And there is more."

"More?!"

"We are going to walk in and out on foot."

"Oh, my God!"

"For the whole world to see!"

"Oh, my God!"

"I know. Either that or..."

"You want me to get shot?"

She whitewashed the risk: "Why? Is Justino the type to shoot someone?"

He and Justino were associates in an incredibly lucrative business venture: Disposing of cadavers produced by the local militias as well as various other sources.

They used the Solace for All funeral home as a front. It had branches in Sao Paulo, in Minas Gerais, and they were thinking of covering the entire southern part of the country.

The concept of "quality" was Solace's trademark. Up to this point, their greatest achievement had been the disposal of Eliza Samudio's[8] body, a true masterpiece by Solace Belo Horizonte. Adalberto suggested Justino make the trip so he could personally make their congratulations to the Belo Horizonte branch, but that was just a pretext for him to spend time with Luci.

Extremely careful, walking on eggs shells—who knows if someone already had informed Justino and he would be looking for Adalberto to settle the accounts—he was startled, "Hey! Weren't you only supposed to come tomorrow?"

Justino smiled gently and, more saintly than ever, "Surprise!"

Adalberto only managed to mutter, "Surprise?"

"Joaquina, my mother in law."

---

8 A famous murder mistery from the year 2010. A soccer player was indicted, but there was no proof. The body has never been found.

"What's going on?"
"Her birthday."
"What!?"
"I bought a present."
"Ah!"
"Want to see?"

Adalberto could not stare him in the eyes. He invented some excuse and practically ran out onto the sidewalk. He felt stalked by Justino's purity, raising the hairs on the back of his neck like the hot breath of the unrelenting enforcer in a Spaghetti Western.

The phone call

That night, Adalberto, who always went to bed early and slept like a rock, managed only a few winks of sleep—and only when the image of Justino stopped tormenting him. The phone awakened him from one of them. It was Luci, who whispered in a titillating voice, "Don't forget tomorrow."

"What about it?"

"Same time, same place."

While still at the hourly motel, she had made him promise.

"But Justino is here. He arrived ahead of schedule."

"It's my mother's birthday. We are returning from her house."

"Right. And then what..."

Silence followed. In that fatal interval, Adalberto could compare the two rascalities, hers and his. Which was worse? Here was Luci, at almost two in the morning, returning with her husband from her mother's birthday party, now demanding a *rendez-vous* from her lover.

Meanwhile, sweet Justino would be placidly dropping his dentures into a glass at the side of their bed.

Not even Messalina! Not even her!

Theorem

The following day, while journeying to Solace, Adalberto had the conviction of a Judas: He was stabbing a just man.

And if it was because of this just man that he was himself stabbed, simple arithmetic ruled that it was fair if the first just man took double stabbings. Therefore, he was not only Judas. He was much more. He was Judas multiplied by two.

Having done the math, Adalberto readied himself to pay for his crime. But how? What had appeared easy at first now sounded impossible. For example, the Biblical Judas undressed his soul of sin by hanging himself from a fig tree. But the center of Campo Grande held not even the shadow of a humble fig.

How, then?

It came to him in a flash. The lack of this tree or that tree was of no importance. Adalberto would undergo a different sort of undressing.

As in the old Pasolini movie, he took off his clothes as he walked. First came the jacket, then the shirt, followed by the trousers, and then the underpants. He left his shoes and socks on because of the bunions on both big toes.

Like this—stripped naked, tears in his eyes and his winky waving in the breeze—he entered Solace, and threw himself at Justino's feet: "Forgive me! Forgive me!"

Astonished, Justino didn't know what to do. Adalberto now embraced his legs. Then Justino bent over and hugged him. They remained like that, embracing each other—Justino with the unconsciousness of the pure, Adalberto with the burning conscience of the impure—until finally someone separated them.

Soon they brought clothes for Adalberto, and soon he released Justino and those who encircled them.

Then he called Luci to confirm their date.

ADRIANA

"**S**he is always throwing it in my face, Antenor.

"What?"

"I already said."

"Say it again."

"But…"

"Repeat it, or else I won't believe you."

Alfredinho, lowering his eyes, whispered, "You are disgusting. Disgusting. Do you hear me?"

"She says that?"

"Every blessed day, when I leave for work and as soon as I step foot in the house."

It was the absolute truth. Adriana stood at the door, hands on her hips, and told him what was to her a transcendental truth.

The whole neighborhood backed her up:

"Exactly right, my daughter. Times have

changed. These days, a man needs a whipping every day, like the old folks said, not to mention that other thing."

That "other thing" alluded to their love life, which to Alfredinho, by the way, amounted to zero—poor guy, so needy, so hungry for care, for sex—but, truly, only with her.

"That's what's killing you, my friend," said Antenor.

"What are you suggesting?"

"Find someone else. A woman can't think she is the only one."

"Someone else? No way!"

"Open your eyes, man."

This irritates Alfredinho.

"Insinuating again, Antenor? For God's sake, stop. Let's change the subject."

The only son of evangelicals, since childhood Alfredinho was protected by his parents, who, along with the Lord, formed a Holy Trinity, and always guarded him from all the world's evils.

With a spiritual purity given to him by these parents and by the Savior, he got married, faced a year and a half of marriage, until...

"You never suspected anything?" asked Antenor.

Alfredinho shrugged. He did not mistrust her, nor could he. In his eyes Adriana was purity personified. She had passed his parents' harsh inspection when their relationship began. The old folks' verdict was final:

"She is virtuous."

That gave the seal of approval to the three month old relationship, followed by the engagement of two months, all without one sign of discord, estrangement, or scratch.

The honeymoon proceeded just as smoothly with the minor exception that Adriana revealed herself to have the temper of a volcano, not at all expected from the timid young woman who sang in the Progressive Evangelical choir and did not permit even so much as a passionate kiss during the engagement.

When the honeymoon ended, she showed even more fireworks: "Wear my panties."

"What are you saying? That's nuts!"

"Pretend you're a little girl."

"Oh, for God's sake, Adriana! Have pity!" he refused, both scandalized and frightened, until one day she committed the fatal blasphemy:

"Let me tie you up in bed. Let me beat you with the clothes line,give you a beating. Like they did to him."

"Him who?"

"Jesus!"

Antenor's eyes opened wide, and he tried to cover an involuntary tremor of his lower lip.

"She asked this of you, did she?"

"Believe it or not."

"What's wrong with that?" The neighbor interjected.

"Do you need to ask?" Alfredinho challenged her.

She didn't play innocent: "Why, is it a crime?"

"A fetish!" blurted Antenor, his voice unmistakably greedy, his breathing now uneven and panting. He remembered the afternoons spent with the couple, there in the living room: she, innocently serving him coffee; he, trying not to stare at her hips, her tits, her ass. Ah. Such blind and dumb naiveté.

After Alfredinho had firmly rebuffed her, Adriana changed. Now she denied him everything, even the right to speak to him, except to repeat that horrible statement.

"Look, if you want to, I can speak with her," Antenor offered.

"And say what?" Alfredinho replied, his voice hard. Had he noticed Antenor's lust?

"I'll speak with her!" the neighbor chimed in, also guessing what Antenor had on mind.

"Wait... I think we need do..." muttered the father, his conscience carrying the burden of his faulty evaluation and feeling responsible for his son's unhappiness. His mother tried to remain objective:

"Do you think it is possible to live with such disregard for the love of Jesus?"

"Then why don't you get a divorce?" asked the neighbor, saying what his mother could not bring herself to say.

Alfredinho stared at the woman:

"I can't live without her."

"Yes, but..." the father began.

The front door banged open, announcing Adriana's arrival. They exchanged glances, each person swallowing their words and trying not to choke on them.

What could they do with her standing right in front of them?

That night, Alfredinho waited until she had fallen asleep, crept into the kitchen, grabbed a bottle of alcohol. In the bedroom he doused her body and struck a match.

His face burned by love, pain and horror, he stayed by her side until nothing remained but a small, smoldering stump.

THE ATTACK

Taken completely by surprise he exclaimed:

"Jaime?"

"That's all they talk about."

"Are you sure?"

"Absolutely. It's even been on TV, Datena's program."[9]

"But why?"

"No one knows for sure. They say it was a crime of passion. Or maybe political rivalry.

"And how is Marta?"

"Completely overwhelmed. Who wouldn't be?"

"Haven't seen her in a long time. Is she still beautiful?"

"And very doable."

"She's out of our league, though. Shame."

---

9 A sensationalist journalist

The wedding

The in-laws from the two greatest fortunes in Campo Grande embraced and smiled. Aurelio, Marta's father, owns three bus companies. Erval, Jaime's father, is the owner of the major educational center in the West Zone.

"This marriage unites the bourgeoisie and the proletariat," announced Arandir, the master of ceremonies, in his toast to the newlyweds.

Everyone—scores of guests that were gathered at the main campus of the university on Caroba Road—watched the two old men.

The bombastic Arandir, concludes his speech:

"And uniting under the name that will end the class struggle in Campo Grande, in all of Rio de Janeiro and perhaps elsewhere, our candidate for state legislature, Jaime de Souza."

The honeymoon

The honeymoon was truly sad, in the specially decorated condo in Caxambu,

Hours before the couple's departure, Isabel, Marta's close friend, came to meet with the bride. Locked in the bedroom, they were engaged in a very secret conversation.

"You consider me your friend, don't you? Absolutely trustworthy?" Isabel started, funeral bells tolling in her voice.

"Jesus! Are you trying to scare me?"

"No, but this is serious!"

"I don't want to know!"

"Here's the story," and she stopped, pausing for breath. "Listen, you have never heard anything to make you mistrust Jaime?"

"Like what? I know everything about him."

"Everything?"

"Every little thing."

"Then tell me, what is going on between him and the priest?"

"What priest?"

"Why, Father Eustaquio."

"Envious snake! Evil eye! She sought you out for that!" sputtered Jaime.

"Then answer me. What is between you and the priest?"

"The ex-priest. He took off the cassock a long time ago."

"The Church demanded it. He had no vocation," said Isabel.

"Liar! He requested it because, because…" Jaime stammered.

Isabel finished:

"Because you two were to move in together. In the apartment you bought in his name, in installments, to avoid suspicion. On Uiraquitã Road."

"Oh my, if that's true," groaned Marta.

"You can believe it."

Marta began to wring her hands in misery. But, all of a sudden…

"Wait a sec! How do you happen to know all of this?"

Isabel remained calm. She even smiled and consoled her friend by patting her on the back.

"You can trust me. Keep your eyes open! Watch out!"

Desperate, Marta speaks on the phone:

"What do I do, father?"

"Anything but interrupt the honeymoon. Think of appearances, the scandal, the campaign. Don't forget about that."

"This marriage is over, father."

"No, it is not."

"For me it is. You are still talking about the honeymoon?"

The old man spoke with all the wisdom of a former truck driver, "A good wife knows how to suck it up."

"Send a car to pick me up. I am in no condition to drive."

"No way. Sleep in the other bedroom, but don't leave. I'm going to find Erval. Cool off. We'll find a way out of this."

Before the old man hung up, Marta had a flash of insight: "There is only one way to forget all this, father."

"What way is that?"

"I'll suck it up if he…"

And she paused almost long enough to give the old man a heart attack.

"Speak! If he what?"

"Withdraws from the campaign."

Setting things straight

"Look, Aurelio, I'm going to be straight with you."

"I'm waiting."

"I think Marta is being a sissy."

"Excuse me, but if anyone is a sissy in this story, it's your son."

"Do you have any concrete proof?"

"Well…what if Isabel…"

Erval, with a wicked smile said,

"Do you believe what she said? Huh? Do you?"

Facing the other's silence, Erval stammered:

"I'll go even further. Do you believe this Isabel even exists? Then answer this: When have you ever seen her? Does she have a CPF,[10] an identity card, a driver's license? Huh?"

"Well, in fact I have never seen her, but…"

Erval raises his finger: "Still we are going to admit the possibility. It's an hypothesis, only for the sake of argument, that she exists, that she is made of flesh and blood. But has she told the truth?"

"What is your point?"

"My point is that Marta's price is very high. Damn it."

"Stop right there! Calm down! Who is saying that my daughter is for sale?"

"Excuse me. I meant to better say, her forgiveness is. Way too expensive."

"Well, then."

"That's what I thought. But…" Now he paused for tremendous effect. "I have a solution! Worthy of Solomon!"

"What is it?"

In one breath, Erval:

"Marta forgets what she asked and Jaime forgets that any such priest exists. We're even. Easy as that. So? Deal?"

---

10 Brazilian Social Security number.

Eustáquio

The agreement only worked for Jaime and the old men.

For the old men it worked because the campaign was in full sail.

As for Jaime... well, he would now act with impudence toward the agreement. From the beginning, while on the campaign trail, he showed off his wife with an attitude that only the completely happy can exhibit.

In the streets of Campo Grande and at other campaign stops, the performance was even more exaggerated. She heard comments: "Yes, sir. The marriage was good for her. She is even hotter."

She felt like screaming, but the figure of Eustaquio paralyzed her, like a terrifying Exu.[11]

Maybe it was because of the Exu, or because of everything else, but she found her husband more and more disgusting as time passed, especially when she thought about him being with the priest...

Then, with the fury of a leper, she would rub her cheeks to remove the kisses he had planted on her for the campaign pictures.

One morning, as soon as she opened her

---

11 A voodoo devil.

eyes—they now slept in widely separated beds—
she became obsessed by the unsettling idea
that Jaime and Eustaquio had married. In the
church. With a white dress and veil, showered by
rice and everything...

That was the last straw. Clearly Eustaquio
had come out on top, but that didn't give him a
license to trample...

If Jaime's happiness scorned her, Eustaquio's did so even more. But, damn! How had
it come to this? This was a slippery slope. She
needed to do something.

The surprise

She found the person's name in the classi-
fied section of the paper. She called, he showed
up. His first impression did not inspire trust,
leading her to ask:

"Are you really a private detective?"

The guy talked like a young punk. He
hardly knew Campo Grande; and, to make matters worse, he chewed his gum while he talked.

"It's out of habit, lady, and also because of
the apnea."

"Trouble breathing, huh?"

"Yeah, smoking. I'm trying to stop."

"Well..."

She decided to take her chances. She gave him all of the information, appointments, itineraries, everything about Jaime. And she was quite explicit about what she wanted him to uncover.

"You say he takes the day off every Friday…"

"No, not the whole day off. He takes care of campaign commitments, the pay, managing the campaign, those things. Then he stays until late playing biriba[12] with the staff."

"Biriba, huh?"

"Uh huh."

"An innocent game, right?"

He smiled knowingly and left.

She didn't hear from him for three days. She began to think she had made something out of nothing and had lost her money—he'd charged her half by the day and the other half at the completion of the investigation, but she paid everything at their first meeting. Then he showed up.

"Didn't I tell you?"

"What?"

"The card game, the biriba, lady."

"What about it?"

"It's all recorded here."

He handed her the cell phone with pic-

---

12 A card game

tures of Jaime's car parked in front of a nondescript building. Jaime entered. The image faded. Marta turned to the detective, who said:

"Wait a second."

The image reappeared.

"Now he is returning. Two hours later."

He hugged a woman and walked toward the car.

The detective zoomed in on the woman. The picture showed Jaime passionately kissing Isabel. He got in the car and left as she stood on the sidewalk waving good-bye, throwing him kisses, and then went inside.

The film ended. Marta put her hand on her heart, groaned, and fainted.

The detective shook his head in resignation. He still hadn't shown her the other video, the one with the priest. He waited a little while, then gave up, left an envelope by her side containing a copy and a large number of photos, and left.

The revenge

In a phone booth, Marta dials Eustaquio's number. Disguising her voice, she says that he was being betrayed, that Jaime has a lover in Bangu, gave the address, the days, the times of the meetings, and such.

A couple of times, he yelled.

"Who is speaking? Who is this?"

Before hanging up, she added that he could rest easy, that Jaime's wife was a poor wretch who didn't know anything and had not a clue.

She lies down at home. She had no idea how much time had passed when she heard knocking on the door. She opened it, and her father and father-in-law entered, breathing heavily. Her father took her in his arms, saying, "You need to be strong, my daughter."

And her father-in-law:

"An attack with political motivations."

Again the father:

"It is a time for deep reflection."

And went on to tell her what happened.

She lowers her head and turns her face away. She tries to control the laughter, but it is too hard; and when her father says that this was a colossal tragedy, with two almost-fatal victims thus far, she bursts into an uncontrolled, depraved, self-satisfied roar.

THE EYE OF THE LORD

Ariovaldo never tired of repeating:

"Listen, we were born guilty. Happiness is an aberration. It ought to be prohibited. There should be posters everywhere, advertising. The only purification is through suffering."

He reiterated his conviction:

"The eye of the Lord! That's how he wanted it! He keeps his eye on us all the time!"

The mother used to cry:

"I have to carry this cross. Who knows from whom he learned this."

Oscar, the close friend, tried to ponder:

"Ari, listen up!" He was the only one who could treat him like this, due to their closeness. "This makes no sense. Forget about it. Snap out of it. Wake up, man!"

Meditative, Ariovaldo answered:

"The eye of the Lord! The eye!"

It wouldn't surprise anyone that his life was as arid as the Sahara desert. And the first and closest victim, not counting his mother, was his girlfriend.

Leonor

Both were salespeople at the Ponto Frio store on the Campo Grande strip: He in the home appliances section, she, in the bath and bedding department. Ariovaldo demanded from Leonor the same convictions, therefore transforming their relationship into a lunar landscape.

"I don't know how you stand it, Jesus!" said the neighbor.

Leonor agreed, but hoped:

"He will change. I am sure."

"Positive?"

"Everyone changes some day, don't they?"

Ariovaldo's mother shrugged her shoulders:

"That dog won't hunt, daughter. You know what he's up to now? Do you?"

She answered her own question:

"He is trying to found a new religion."

"You're joking!" exclaimed Oscar.

Leonor sighed deeply. In truth, despite having the patience of Job—if the Biblical figure had a woman's face, it would be hers—almost a year into the relationship and with the promise of an engagement, she was already getting fed up.

After all, not very tall but exuberantly endowed, she awoke the most primal desires in any man.

"Except Ariovaldo. Can you believe it?" she asked Oscar, who was, by the way, the manager of the shop and her confidante.

"Tremendous injustice! Tremendous injustice!" he exclaimed, eyeing the sultry young woman and dumb-founded at Ariovaldo's stupidity.

"I feel humiliated, I am sad to say."

"Very sad."

"But I feel that way."

"Poor thing!"

Oscar came out of this chat feeling broken and with the firm conviction that Ariovaldo was the biggest jackass in the world. But he was not. Nope. No siree.

Cellar rat

"I won't take no for an answer. No way. I want to be the best man," said Ariovaldo.

Oscar's face lowered into a frown. He was ready for anything, except this, so much so that before he met him, he had to consult with Ariovaldo's mother.

"And how should I know how he is going to react?"

"I am only asking your opinion, Dona Dolores. You understand, don't you? The subject is a little delicate."

"A little?!"

Oscar was one of those grumpy old bastards whose conscience never suffered a twinge. To be honest, he consulted with the old lady only out of fear of taking a bullet to his head.

He knew Ariovaldo well and knew he was incapable of such a thing; but, like any good scoundrel, he understood human nature and always feared the reactions of the calm.

As a matter of fact, he would not take any action at all if it weren't for Leonor demanding it and responding in a whisper:

"I cannot say. This is killing me. It is you who must do that."

"As if I didn't already know. Relax, Oscar. You think I'm blind? Do you?"

And he repeated:

"When you get married, I want to be the best man. Truly," and he smiled with such peacefulness that it made Oscar feel like a rat in the cellar.

The death

The life of Oscar and Leonor was sailing along, swimmingly. One could say they were living the dream.

And if that wasn't enough, the lucky devil won the lottery, not the grand prize, but enough to consider quitting his job at Ponto Frio and setting up his own business.

But one cursed Tuesday morning a bomb exploded on his Hollywood musical set: Ariovaldo died.

"Like a little bird, without even a peep!" moaned Dona Dolores at the wake.

Then, her mind wandered:

"Last night, he ate a little bowl of hominy and went to sleep."

Then turning to Oscar:

"Do you know anyone who died from eating hominy?"

It has already been told that Oscar was a scoundrel. The simple truth. But a scoundrel that gave minimal support. He even questioned having to pay half of the funeral.

"What the…Pay it all! Didn't you just win the lottery?" whispered Leonor, looking even sadder than Dona Dolores.

"I am thinking of our future, baby. In the

end no one knows what tomorrow will bring, right?

But at the cemetery he gave a tip to the gravediggers. At the marble works in front, he recommended a bigger tombstone and would have done more if Leonor, hanging on his arm, had not said, "The eye."

"What eye?"

"Of the Lord."

"What about it?"

"I can see it."

"You're kidding! Where?"

"Without hearing him, she repeated, like an echo,

"The eye! The eye!"

Deeply concerned, he prevented her from seeing the body being lowered in the grave. He took her home. There, a neighbor made her orange-blossom tea. Between sips, she fixed her eyes on Oscar:

"A shame, our happiness."

Wringing her hands:

"Ariovaldo was a saint. We killed him. It was us."

Requital

The following day, the neighbor called

him at work.

"Mister Oscar?"

"What happened?"

"Leonor..."

"Yes. What happened?"

"It's that... Well..."

"Tell me."

"Look, it would be better if you came here."

"But..."

"Come right away, Mister Oscar."

He only had time to throw on a jacket and run out the door. In front of the house he ran into some neighbors with their heads together, whispering. They clammed up as soon as they saw him, respectfully stepping back to let him through.

Oscar entered the house and took a deep breath. In the middle of the living room sat a large, black casket, its lid closed. Beside it burned four long candles. Black drapes covered the windows. At the far end of the room—dark, somber, and filled with the sickening smell of the candles—knelt Leonor, facing the wall. Dressed in black from head to toe, she formed a figure so tragic, he stopped dead in his tracks.

When he had recovered enough to announce his arrival, a neighbor took him by the arm:

"It won't help. She has been like this since the casket arrived. Her last words were that she would never again speak to anyone, not even to Dona Dolores. Much less to you."

Then Oscar understood. Leonor had closed herself off and was waiting to die by purging all of the happiness she had felt when he was with her. When all was said and done, Ariovaldo had won the game. By going to the grave, he took revenge. Dead, Ariovaldo meant more than Oscar, who was right there, alive and kicking.

A good loser, he took one final look at Leonor, gave a roguish smile, and, already welcoming the joys of a widower, he left.

He passed the neighbors still at the door, whistling a song by Zeca Pagodinho[13]. He did not return to work. In a corner bar he drank a beer and watched a rerun of the Flamengo-Fluminense soccer game on TV, the game he had missed because of Ariovaldo's funeral.

---

13 Pop music singer.

PANTALEONE

At the peak of his fury, Teixeira yelled:

"Now there is nothing left to do but shoot her!"

And he repeated, without even showing any regard for Isaura's palpitations:

"I have to shoot her. Where is she?"

"Stop!"

"Where is she? In her room?"

Throwing herself at his feet, Isaura begged:

"Don't you go in there! Don't!"

Pushing her away, he freed himself and left, silently smoldering in anger.

The meeting

When he saw her, Teixeira was buying Italian salami at Sendas Supermarket, near the overpass. He liked her type. She reminded him of an old passion: ripe, brown-skinned, medium-tall, and what a body.

He made his approach:

"Are you single, married, or *tico-tico-no-fubá*[14]?"

She smiled. He followed, insidiously:

"Do I have a chance? Big or little?"

Always smiling, she answered his first question:

"Married. Why?"

"I love it."

"A married woman?"

"A husband is not always a good defense. When he stops being..."

"So, it's time for another man?"

Now it was he who was smiling. He had gained a grand slam advantage over his former sweetheart.

Then things happened as fast as they do in a TV series. Before he knew it they were riding in his car; ten minutes later they entered the presidential suite of the Salou Motel on Mendanha Road.

The truth is that when she saw him in the checkout line, she felt very nervous, defenseless. It was as if she were being raped right there,

---

14 Reference to the Brazilian samba singer, Broadway actress and Hollywood film star Carmen Miranda's 1947 song "Tico Tico".

standing, squeezed against the grocery cart. Astonished by her frailty as a woman, she was not able to control herself.

In desperation, she thought, *My God! Why don't I ever feel these things with Adalberto? Why?*

Now, at the hourly motel, it was too late. She gave herself to Teixeira with the fury of a wild boar at the zoo.

Mother's love

The mother, babalorixá,[15] and moral authority of the Corcundinha neighborhood, said with merciless cruelty:

"After fifteen years of marriage, no woman has the right to cheat."

The neighbor, with the air of an accomplice, said:

"Tremendous ingratitude."

And Isaura said,

"Only if one is still in love."

"Don't you love me anymore?" Adalberto wanted to know.

"No more than you love me."

The neighbor says,

"It goes without saying that this Teixeira...I don't know..."

---

15 A Candomble (African religion) priestess.

The mother, curious:

"What about him?"

With the cold detachment of a forensic pathologist dissecting a cadaver, the neighbor chronicled, blow by blow, Teixeira's amorous escapades.

On his behalf, the mother invoked the support of the most unusual and powerful Orishas. And with the gravity of someone intimate with such entities said,

"And what about little Tina? Did you think of her?"

"You can go. She stays with me," Adalberto moaned, his voice shaking, with the agitation of the betrayed.

Isaura smiled:

"Teixeira has already met her. He loves her."

The neighbor also smiled, maliciously:

"He has hidden intentions."

Surrogate father

"Imagine! A second father! The father she never had is what I want to be."

And he was, but a conservative father, older than Methuselah.

The truth is that sixteen year-old Tina

possessed the beauty of a Florentine Madonna, or as they said when they still read Nabokov, she was the perfect Lolita. Naturally, Teixeira approached her with utmost care.

Except he went overboard. When some young guy showed an interest, he researched his background; and at the first opportunity, he would approach him and demand that they see each other only at home, this kind of thing.

Meaning, the ex-dissolute now expected from others a sacrosanct rectitude. He condemned Tina to an unfortunate future as an alluring spinster. Most curiously, she appeared to realize this, but not to mind.

Columbine

Then the indescribable happened, a true Dantesque tragedy.

To purge his former and lascivious orgies, it was Teixeira's habit to travel with his family during Carnival to the quiet Piquara Beach, in Mangaratiba, staying at the inn run by his friend, Emil de Castro.

It happened that mischievous Tina slipped a strong dose of barbiturates in their food so she could leave and party until dawn at Club Mangarás, always surrounded by a swarm of satyrs.

It was only on the last night that Teixeira, attacked by a banal case of heartburn, discovered the subterfuge when he got up for a glass of milk. He ran into Tina in the hall as she returned from the club, wearing a scandalous Columbine costume.

"Ay!" she yelled, and ran to her room.

For a long time, Teixeira stood in the middle of the hallway, paralyzed. When he recovered from the shock, he went looking for Emil. He wanted an explanation. After all, Tina could hardly go in and out like that unless his friend...

Emil said he perfectly understood his friend's anxiety, and if he were in his shoes he would...blah blah blah, but Teixeira should also understand his position, which was that maybe Tina had bribed someone at the entrance or something. Anyway, he didn't know anything.

"Accomplice!" accused Teixeira.

"What?!"

In his frenzy, Teixeira again accused, "Accomplice! You!"

In the face of his friend's silence, Teixeira cut loose with the ultimate insult:

"Scoundrel!"

"I am not."

Emil assumed the impressive posture of an old, experienced Indian chief. And he rose in deathly peacefulness:

"As a matter of fact, I would a thousand times rather be a scoundrel than a dumb, old Pantaleone."

Teixeira wilted. With his enviable cultural literacy, Emil reduced him to a mere scratch, a burnt match.

With his tail between his legs, but fuming with anger, he turned his back and went to his room. He entered, enraged, yelling at the top of his voice:

"Now I have to shoot her!"

Isaura, who had heard everything through a crack in the door, felt a pang in her chest:

"Ouch!"

"Where is she? In her room?"

And Isaura, falling to the ground and grabbing his legs:

"Don't you go in there! Don't!"

Pushing her away, he freed himself and left, fuming in unspoken frustration.

Settling accounts

He entered Tina's room and, suddenly sweet, said:

"My daughter, listen---"

"I am not."

"Not what?"

"Not your daughter."

"But…"

"I don't even want to be. To tell you the truth, I never did."

"Wait, I…"

"Do you think I don't know? Huh? Do you?"

"Think what?"

"That you…"

"You've always treated me with respect. Why are you doing this now?"

"I don't respect you."

"No?"

"Not at all. You do not deserve it."

"Since I married your mother, I have treated you like a daughter…"

"You liar! You treat me like the lover you would like to have."

"No, I don't!"

"You always wanted to sleep with me. Your eyes don't lie, the way your mouth twitches. I've noticed it from the beginning."

"Wait! Listen…"

"My boyfriends…"

"They wanted to take advantage of you. I defended you."

"They were sixteen. I slept with all of them."

"No!"

"Did you know I laughed behind your back?"

"No, no, no!"

"And now…"

"What's happened?"

"You came in here only to sleep with me."

"You lie!"

"Come on! I'm waiting!"

"No! No!"

"I confess. You know what? I want you too. Since the day of your wedding. At night I heard you and my mother. I was listening at your bedroom door."

"You were?"

"When I couldn't have you, I gave myself to others. Revenge, you see. I needed to get even by hurting myself.

"But now…"

"Come. Why are you wasting time?"

"Your mother…"

"She cuckolded my father. Now I am going to put the horns on her. It is destiny. You get what you deserve."

"Cover your thighs."

"You don't like them?"

"Those tits."

"You don't like them?"

"Yes, I like them. I love them!"

"Come, Daddy. Come."

Teixeira hurled himself on top of her with the fervor of a mountain goat in the rut. It was the last thing he ever did.

No one understood why Tina didn't go to the funeral, much less why she locked herself in the house and yelled, scaring the neighbors, pulling her hair, asking to die too.

Equally hard to fathom was why Teixeira's corpse appeared so healthy. Many even commented that they'd never seen a dead man who was so elegant and handsome.

In fact, he emitted a strong but incomprehensible vitality, a happiness, as if only in death Teixeira found the type of peace exuded by saints—a true, inescapable, pure peace.

VIRAGO

They meet on the boardwalk. Durvalino pulls him to a corner:

"Anacleto, listen. You're my friend, right?"

"Do you need to ask?"?"

"You swear?"

"I'll ask it again. Do you doubt it?"

Durvalino took a deep breath. And after a dramatic pause:

"Listen. I'm going to make a confession, something really serious."

Then, standing close enough to splatter his face with spit:

"But this stays just between us. Promise?"

"I swear."

"I don't trust Isaurinha. She is cheating on me."

"Oh, Durvalino, for God's sake! She's totally faithful!"

"Yeah, right!"

"What?"

"The crafty ones. The most dangerous."

"But Isaurinha…"

"Besides being crafty, she's deceitful. I repeat: a dreadful danger."

"Facts. Proofs. Do you have any?"

"Signs."

"But then…"

"Highly compromising."

"Like what?"

"A half hour in front of the mirror before she goes out shopping for groceries; hair dresser three times a week; joined a Gym."

"But, Durvalino, that's not…"

"Want some more?"

He lowered his voice:

"Every day, always at the same time: a phone call. If I answer it, no one speaks. I just hear breathing, heavy, lascivious breathing, to be precise. If she answers, she chats forever."

"But Durvalino, listen, pay attention…"

"To cut this conversation short, I'll give you *carte blanche*. Entirely yours."

"Whoa, to do what?"

"Can't you guess?"

"No."

"To flirt with Isaurinha, see if she falls for your lines."

"But, Durvalino! Hit on your wife? That is what you're asking? From a friend?"

"Who am I going to ask, an enemy? The only thing is… don't go all the way with her."

"All the way?!"

"To consummation. Do you understand?"

And before Anacleto could reply, with his finger pointing, Durvalino said,

"I am counting on you. Take care of this, ok?"

He turned and disappeared into the crowd.

Indigestible friend

The sad truth was that Anacleto just couldn't stand such weirdness any longer.

"It is too heavy, understand?" He had vented to another friend, Brito down to the last detail. "Durval is a leech, almost a cancer. He devours people."

Almost fifteen days ago he had taken him by the arm and told him, with the tone of a bum:

"I may kick the bucket within a week."

"Why?"

"An illness. Fatal."

"You're kidding."

"Dr. Alberto guaranteed it."

"Alberto, huh?"

"I want you to take care of everything: funeral service, burial, I'll leave you the money for my cemetery plot, which is overdue. But above all, I want you to take care of Isaurinha. Can I count on you?"

As it happened, over the course of the week the fatal illness was forgotten, the death was forgotten even more, and then came again Durvalino with his...

Isaurinha

Anacleto was thinking of these things as he walked to the bus station to catch a bus, when who passed in front of him? Isaurinha herself.

She looked, as they used to say, uglier than a mud fence.

At school, she never had a boyfriend.

And worse, when she was a young woman, the neighbors would say:

"She has no future. Who the hell would take her?"

"Her father is rich."

Then Durval appeared.

"This guy isn't from Campo Grande."

"He looks like a poor immigrant."

And the most improbable marriage happened.

"Married her for the money."

"Got a big house with a pool and every-thing, a present from the old man."

"Not counting the business. He won the lottery."

Seeing Isaurinha walking away—well dressed, it is true, but still terribly ugly—Ana-cleto was absolutely certain that Durvalino was delirious again. Then, solemnly, he quit thinking about it.

U-turn

At night, however, in the drowsiness be-fore sleep, he found himself thinking about it again. And Anacleto reconsidered. He remem-bered the words of Brito:

"Someone marries a rich woman and im-mediately becomes important. Whereas, people like us..."

Brito was one of those heard-hearted hick guys, resenting his lack of success in business.

This ate away at Anacleto too. He, like Brito, resented these injustices. Theoretically, he had everything—good looks, gift of gab, air of confidence—but he never rose beyond an ass-kissing, low-level manager in a little nuts-and-bolts store.

And Durvalino? Without any real charm, he just had the guts to con his way into a marriage of convenience. And he flaunted it in front of everyone. Was that fair? Did it not merit corrective action?

"Indeed it does. Go for it, man. Don't just flirt, give him a beautiful pair of horns. Go for it," the indefensible Brito urged.

Intimate

Anacleto began to visit the couple, won their confidence, and received Isaurinha's good graces.

Eventually, he discovered wicked things. For example, Durvalino was rough with his wife. Isaurinha, who, on the other hand, had the delicacy of an ornament. And she possessed the soul of an artist. She was a major second-rate star in the outskirts.

Her resumé would make a person's jaw drop: poetess, writer, painter, regular columnist in the Seropedica paper, another in a Campo Grande paper, published books, showings of her paintings both in Campo Grande and abroad, membership in the Campo Grande Institute of Culture, a literary blog on the internet. She had done it all.

Curiously, Anacleto's eyes no longer saw Isaurinha as ugly:

It is internal beauty that matters.

All of that made him arrive at the obvious conclusion that he was in love with her.

And the sweet-talk? The desire to avenge himself on Durvalino? It was imperative that he give all that up. He would do it in the name of love. He would do even more: as a punishment for the ignominy he had planned to perpetrate, he would stop seeing her. He would renounce forever basking in her radiant inner light.

And, to make his punishment more severe than justice would require, he began to think of moving from Campo Grande when, one afternoon, he ran into Durvalino, who was looking for him at the nuts-and-bolts store.

A clarifying talk

"Hey, man! You disappeared. What happened?

Anacleto tried to act natural:

"Nothing. I mean…"

After clearing his throat:

"Look, I wanted to tell you I am calling the whole thing off."

"What do you mean?"

"That thing you asked me to do."

"The flirting?"

"I stopped."

"Was she receptive?"

"No."

"Lack of persistence? You had the time, the opportunity, everything."

"I didn't even try, Durvalino."

"Why?"

"Let it go. Forget about it."

"No way."

"It's better that way."

"I insist."

Anacleto averted his eyes:

"It's just that I...well...I fell in love with Isaurinha."

"You did?"

"Madly."

"And..."

He looked him in the eye:

"Nah! Is that all? Don't you want to jab me?"

"Not for that reason, no."

After a brief pause, he took a breath:

"Listen, you think I don't know what everybody says about me?"

"What's that?"

"About my marrying her for the money...

and a hell lot else."

"Well..."

"I must tell you that it's all true, completely true."

"If you say so..."

"Except there is one other thing no one knows. And now I'm telling you. I married Isaurinha out of pure hate. I hated to have to marry a rich woman. The money, Anacleto, is a disgrace, a total disgrace.

And after a third breath:

"The sweet-talking was meant to show her that. In the end, I wanted her to fall in love with you, to love someone. Because I'm certain that she doesn't like me. I know my place, Anacleto. What woman could possibly like a guy like me? She only accepted me to have a husband. It was I who was used, you understand? Me!"

In a choking voice:

"I only wanted to avenge myself! That's all!"

He finished, desperate:

"Do I not have the right to do this? Not even this?"

And he broke out into heartfelt tears of pain.

Anacleto embraced him, and his tears. They stayed like this, hugging and in tears, in front of the shop of nuts-and-bolts.

Whoever passed could see the figure of a woman hovering momentarily over them. As an ugly Campo Grande Gioconda, she smiled a redneck smile, as profound, unfathomable and mysterious as her Florentine namesake's.

TONY CURTIS

Afonsinho entered, waited while Edgar finished waiting on a customer, and whispered secretively:

"Just a while ago...they were saying..."

"What?"

"It has been delivered."

Edgar—owner of a haberdashery in the center of Campo Grande, a meeting place for chatting, rumors, and gossip in general—could not prevent a half-smile:

"Really?"

"Olegario has it."

"Is he going to publish it?"

"Oh yeah..."

Olegario possessed a wickedly divine quality. An uninhibited ignoramus, he founded a weekly newspaper, maintained by the collection of blackmail against local bigwigs in particular, and businessmen in general.

"When?"

"It goes out in the next edition."

"The day after tomorrow?"

"Guaranteed. But you know Olegario, don't you?"

Edgar could not hide his smile of delicious malice:

"Everyone knows him... Everyone."

The big stud

More than anything, Faustino shined for his cynicism. At the Club of the Aliados ball, he would try to scandalize the women and provoke the men by saying,

"The honest woman is a major fiction of the poor in spirit."

"Oh, Faustino, for God's sake, do you really believe that?" asked Edgar in front his most frequent *habitués*.

And Faustino, striking the pose of a Campo Grande justice said,

"Not only that. I affirm more—No one can resist my line."

Such claims were only allowed because of his fragile and completely insignificant appearance. He was considered by the other men a second rate clown, The Tramp with a headache. Since they believed the ladies saw him the same way, they imagined themselves perfectly safe from him.

In truth, being a bachelor, he demonstrated no notable amorous conquest which would confer the slightest credibility to what he was saying.

"Until he died."

"Or was killed."

"By a jealous husband, no doubt."

"Wait, didn't he kill himself?"

"That's the first mystery."

"Is there another?"

The fact is that only his death could show what Faustino had been when he was alive—a Cleopatra in jeans.

In his apartment they found letters, notes, declarations of love—enough evidence to have shaken any marriage in Campo Grande and its surroundings, including the neighborhoods of Vila Nova, Oiticica, Lameirão Pequeno, Corcundinha, and Guandu do Sapé, among others.

On his bedside table they found, listed in Faustino's own whimsical handwriting, the names and addresses of all the senders. And, mostly whimsically, he listed them carefully and in alphabetical order. Since he left the list in plain sight, one must suppose he meant for it to be found.

Thus, there existed proof of wrongdoing along with the identities of the wrongdoers. The next step was to publish it. It would be a bomb powerful enough to pulverize Campo Grande.

Rashes

"I don't see why," said Ivone, when Edgar talked to her about it.

They were living a very rare thing—a perfect marriage. They maintained a cordiality that had lasted more than fifteen years of incredible harmony.

He insisted:

"But the list..."

"It really exists?"

"Huh?"

"Did someone see it?"

"Well..."

"You?"

"No, certainly not."

"Afonsinho?"

"No, not him either."

"Did Olegario show it to anyone?"

"He's going to publish it."

"Really?"

"The day after tomorrow."

She smiled slightly:

"Is he?"

"He promised, right?"

"Do you believe him?"

Before he said anything else:

"Is it possible to believe Olegario?"

"True, but…"

He shut his mouth. And she said, quickly,

"Did you see it?"

"What?"

"On the six o'clock news."

"What?"

"Tony Curtis."

"What about him?"

"He died."

"Ah."

"Do you remember him?"

Why is she changing the subject? It's the first time she's done that.

"More or less."

"He was our favorite leading man."

"Yours. Not mine."

Why does she deny the existence of the list? Why does it matter to her?

"Do you remember that movie…"

"Which movie?"

Faustino was her friend too. He used to visit them in their house. Sometimes he came home from the shop and Faustino was already there, sit-

ting on the sofa in the living room, the two talking. He stayed for dinner two or three times a week.

"That one...where he was a plumber... he fixed things in women's homes...entered, then killed them..."

"Ah?"

"Remember?"

"More or less."

Was she comparing Faustino to Tony Curtis? Freudian slip? Huge studs, these two. But if it was so, she and the list...

"And also 'Spartacus'. That one I remember well.

"Remember?

"The final scene. Kirk Douglas kisses Tony Curtis right after he killed him! Wow! There is also that other one that..."

And she continued listing the names of films, plots, these things; he no longer listened, already under a cloud of doubt that made him feel as disgraced as a thoroughbred with a rash.

The End

Edgar pulled Olegario by the coat and said accusingly:

"You! You wrecked my marriage."

"Me?!"

"You and Tony Curtis!"

"What?"

"And also Faustino."

"Well…"

"The list."

"What list?"

"Faustino's."

"But Tony Curtis?"

"He died."

"And what about him?"

"It's that he and Faustino…Damn, don't you get it?"

"No."

"You can't publish it."

"Are you trying to put a muzzle on me?"

"No, I only…"

"I object!"

"Listen, Afonsinho…"

"We have a democracy now."

"I know. I know…"

"But we can arrange it."

"I want to check it beforehand."

"Huh?"

"The list."

"It's worth a lot of money."

"Okay."

"Do you have the money?"

"Do you have the list?"

As soon as he entered the house, Edgar confronted Ivone and said dramatically:

"I died. Are you listening? Died!"

Astonished, she said,

"What are you talking about? What happened?"

He went to the bedroom, locked himself in, put on a black suit, lay down on the bed, crossed his arms over his chest and closed his eyes as if he were bidding goodbye to this world.

www.ingramcontent.com/pod-product-compliance
Lightning Source LLC
Chambersburg PA
CBHW071337130626
46556CB00004B/1925